# THE COURAGEOUS JOURNEY

Success is never without its challenges.

## Wisdom For Real Life
### YouTube Channel

KUSHAL DESAI

Copyrighted Material

The Courageous Journey: Success is never without its challenges.



For any information about this title or any other queries,
Contact the publisher: kushaldesai9012@gmail.com

Cover & Design: Kushal Desai
First Edition: 2023

All characters - in this publication are fictitious and any resemblance to real persons, living or dead, is purely coincidental

# ACKNOWLEDGEMENTS

First and foremost, I want to express my gratitude to my parents Vasantha Madhuri Desai & Kopreshwar Rao Desai, who are always there for me.

A special thanks to my friends who know who I am and what I am.

5

---

*A Quote In Sanskrit*

---

*"You become what you believe.*

*यत् भावो तत् भवति"*

# TABLE OF CONTENTS

11

# INTRODUCTION

Meet Mr. Suraj who lived in a small village in India. The village was surrounded by tall hills and thick forest. The people who lived there often had big dreams, and the village is as pleasant as many parts of India.

Suraj was not just like the other kids in the village. He was passionate, courageous, and had a dream of art.

At Sunset, Suraj was enjoying the pleasing view of the village, and his curiosity led him to walk towards the hills to explore the forest as he was captivated by the tall trees. His thought process was unique, and he had a powerful desire to accomplish something extraordinary in life.

The very next day, Suraj made the decision to enter the forest again but this time it was in the morning. He had a straightforward intention of discovering something new and adopting it as he did not have fancy art supplies. Instead, he used a stick with leaves at the end as his paintbrush.

He created the ultimate work of art on a flat rock. Instead of colourful paints, he utilised leaves, soil, and the sunlight that filtered through the trees.

Suraj was unaware that he was doing something amazing; who would have known at that point? He was creating art to transform ordinary things into beautiful creations. His colours and shapes of his brush strokes made the rock come alive.

What Suraj had discovered was the magic of creating things. He realised that simple things in the world could transform into something that expresses your emotions. It was like he had found a treasure deep inside him that would shine for a long time.

Despite everything, something else happened that day that was even more incredible. Suraj heard soft rustling sounds behind him while painting.

As soon as he turned around, he saw a lady standing there. She was unlike anyone he had ever met, and her name is Chandini. Chandini's face was kind and her eyes seemed to hold all the secrets of the world. She walked up to Suraj, saw his painting, and smiled warmly. Chandini was an artist herself, but she was also like a guardian of the forest.

The most interesting part about Chandini is, she had spent years exploring the woods and sharing what she had learned with those who were willing to listen.

Her attention was drawn to something unique in Suraj's artwork, something that was more than just colour on a rock. After introducing herself, she became Suraj's friend and mentor. She taught Suraj on how to capture the beauty of nature and how to create paintings/art that tell stories and express emotions.

"Isn't that the beauty of art? It conveys our emotions."

However, life in the village was sometimes not easy. One of the tough times was when Chandini got extremely sick. Suraj faced a big challenge – he could give up on his art dreams because of the difficulties around him, or he could use his art to bring hope to the village and to honour Chandini's memory.

The theme of the story is the ability of art to enrich people's lives, along with determination and self-confidence. The story covers plenty of years and many different adventures.

The story of Suraj's growth from a little child with dreams to an established artist, whose paintings inspired individuals all over the world.

Suraj's work will develop and grow as we notice. We'll find out just how he fought in the face of difficulties. We'll see how he supported those around him and recognized the deep impact that art can have on people.

This story is a powerful signal to follow your aspirations, believe in yourself. Remember that even one person can make a significant difference in life.

Reading about Suraj's journey makes us feel like we are starting our own adventure. It conveys the idea that nothing is impossible if we have faith in our abilities and believe in ourselves.

So, let's join Suraj as he starts on his incredible journey. His story is like a vibrant, emotional art. It is a tale of bravery and optimism. And it all starts with one step, which can be done with a hopeful heart.

# CHAPTER 1: A BOY WITH DREAMS

Suraj, a boy who lived in a small village surrounded by hills. He was completely different from other kids. He was thinking about his goals and making plans to achieve them while kids around him were having fun. He had a great deal of passion for making art. Due to their limited financial resources, Suraj's family was unable to buy expensive art tools like colours, brushes, and other supplies.

However, that didn't stop Suraj from continuing. Regardless of anything, he was going to make his art. He would go to the nearby forest every day after school. From there he would gather broken twigs, smooth stones, and colourful leaves.

He started making wonderful paintings by using these basic materials. He was not familiar with various art-making methods, but he did not care.

He was guided by his heart as he made his creations. Each piece stood for a facet of his spirit that was on display.

People in the village would often pass by and watch Suraj's work. Some would laugh, thinking he was wasting his time with his temporary artwork. But some others saw something special in him. They could see the effort and love he put into each piece.

Suraj wished to become a well-known artist. His aim was to share his art with the world and make people feel something when they looked at it.

The dream was big for a boy who lived in a small village. However, he had complete faith in it.

Suraj's painting improved as the days turned into weeks, and the weeks turned into years. He tried out creative methods for using twigs and leaves.

He discovered the ability to mix all kinds of colours from the stones he discovered. He was able to capture the beauty of the environment around him via his artwork.

However, life was not without its difficulties. The family was still struggling, and there weren't always enough meals on the table. Suraj was often worried about his ability to follow his passion without proper art tools. Suraj survived in the face of difficulties. He understood that great art was made by the heart and not by expensive tools. And he put a lot of emotions into his work.

One bright afternoon, while Suraj was making a masterpiece out of a fallen tree branch and vibrant leaves, he met someone who would change his life forever.

# CHAPTER 2: A MEETING WITH CHANDINI

On a bright afternoon, Suraj engaged in his work, and he heard some noise on his back. When he turned around, he noticed a kind elderly woman standing and giving an intent look towards his artwork.

The woman's eyes were twinkling with curiosity and warmth. She smiled at Suraj and said with a soothing voice.

Young man, 'Your art is quite remarkable.' I've never witnessed anything like it.

Suraj was initially surprised by the unexpected company but managed to smile with a shyness.

"Thank you very much, ma'am." "I only use what I can find in the woods."

The woman took a step forward and started looking more closely at his work. She said, "You know, I've seen many artists in my life, but there is a fire in your eyes that is something truly special.

Your work is more than just what you use; it is also about how you feel on the inside. Suraj felt an intense feeling of warmth as he listened to her words. No one had ever understood his art like this before.

The woman introduced herself as Chandini, who has been a long-time resident of the village. Throughout her life, she had many dreams, and Suraj's dedication reminded her of her own childhood ambitions.

Chandini said, 'Suraj, don't let anything stop you,' and her eyes widened on him. "Keep creating and dreaming. Your art has the power to touch people's hearts and make them see the beauty in the simplest things.

Suraj's heart was filled with excitement. Although he didn't know much about Chandini, he could tell that she was wise and caring. She seemed like a person who had seen the world and understood its secrets.

From that day forward, Chandini became Suraj's mentor and friend. She shared stories of her own dreams and the challenges she had faced. She taught him about various art techniques and encouraged him to "dream big".

Suraj's work began to come to life under Chandini's mentoring. He mastered the art of colour blending and texture creation. He felt as if a whole new world had opened for him, and he eagerly embraced it.

Suraj's amazing artwork spread through everyone, and visitors from other towns quickly flocked to see his creations. They were amazed by his ability to turn ordinary materials into works of art and passion. Suraj's dream of being a successful artist was gradually becoming a reality.

But life, as it often does, had one more challenge in store for Suraj. Chandini's health gradually diminished. She became ill, and her strength dropped day by day. Suraj was heartbroken but he refused to give up.

He continued to create art, making every piece a tribute to Chandini. He painted her courage in the face of adversity, her unwavering belief in him, and the moments they had shared under the canopy of the forest.

One evening, as Suraj sat by Chandini's bedside, holding her hand, she spoke to him quietly with a lower pitch.

"You've shown the world that true art comes from the heart, my dear. Keep inspiring others with your passion."

Suraj's eyes were filled with tears as he listened to her words. Chandini was not just a mentor; she was his guiding light and source of inspiration. Her belief in him and his own determination had led him to a place he had never dreamed of.

With Chandini's words echoing in his heart, Suraj knew that if he painted with his heart, his dreams would always come true.

# CHAPTER 3: THE ARTISTIC AWAKENING

With Chandini's guidance, Suraj's art progressed into something truly remarkable. He explored his imagination further by experimenting with colours and textures and finding new methods to express himself via his work.

He would eagerly go to the forest every day and collect materials that spoke to him. Twigs became the sturdy branches of trees in his paintings, leaves were transformed into intricate patterns, and smooth stones gave his work a unique depth.

The villagers, who had once doubted the boy with his invented art supplies, now watched in awe as Suraj's creations came to life.

His art captivated their hearts, capturing the essence of the natural world around them. They realised that art was not about the cost of materials, but about the passion and soul that was poured into every piece.

On a sunny afternoon, Suraj and Chandini sat down under the shade of a tree. They were next to his latest art creation, a clear and powerful depiction of a serene forest. Suraj looked at Chandini and said, I can't thank you enough for believing in me and guiding me,". Suraj's eyes were filled with gratitude. Chandini smiled and her eyes sparkled with wisdom. She said, "Suraj, I've seen many artists in my life, but you have a gift that is truly unique.

"Suraj has never been appreciated like this by Chandini before." She said, your art isn't just beautiful; it's filled with the emotions and dreams of your heart. That's what sets you apart."

Suraj nodded, his heart overflowing with a renewed feeling of purpose. He knew Chandini had shown him a path to being the artist he would always want to be.

As the years went by, Suraj's art continued to develop. He painted landscapes that seemed to come alive, portraits that captured the very essence of his subjects, and abstract pieces that beat the imagination. People from neighbouring towns came to visit the village to see Suraj's skilled work.

Suraj's dream of becoming a successful artist was gradually turning into a reality. However, life had one more challenge in store for him, one that would test his courage and determination in ways he could never have imagined.

# CHAPTER 4: A TEST OF FAITH

During a winter when the village was covered in fog, word spread like lightning speed across the village. Suraj's cherished mentor and friend, Chandini, had become terribly ill. In fact, even more sick than before. Her once lively energy was gone, and her strength became weaker with each passing day.

Suraj rushed to Chandini's side with a heavy heart of worry. He couldn't bear to see her suffering. He wanted to do something to help, to make her better, but he felt helpless. Suraj's eyes were full of tears. He sat down next to Chandini and said, it's hard for me to see you like this.

Chandini's smile was weak, and she whispered, "My dear Suraj, life is filled with tests of faith. This is one of mine.

But remember, you have a gift that has the power to bring light into the darkest of times. Keep sharing your art with the world. It's your passion and love that have touched so many hearts, including mine."

Suraj nodded, his voice dripping with emotion. He couldn't imagine a world without Chandini's wisdom and encouragement.

He left her bedside with a heavy heart. He wanted to do something for Chandini, so he decided to create art that would honour her spirit and strength.

In the days that followed, Suraj painted tirelessly. He poured his emotions into every stroke of his brush, creating masterpieces that reflected Chandini's resilience and the cherished moments they had shared. His art became a tribute to her unwavering belief in him.

The villagers came to support Suraj because they knew about Chandini's health condition. Their support and encouragement reminded him of the impact his art had on their lives.

It was a reminder that art had the power to inspire and uplift, even in the darkest of times.

# CHAPTER 5: A TIMELESS LEGACY

As winter gave way to spring, Chandini's health continued to deteriorate. She remained bedridden. Suraj visited her every day, sharing stories of his art and the people who had been touched by it.

One evening, as the sun cast a warm glow through Chandini's window, she made a gesture with her hand and invited Suraj to her bedside.

Her voice was barely a whisper, but her eyes were full of wisdom and love.

"Suraj," she began, "I've seen you grow from a determined young boy into an aspiring talented artist." You've shown the world that true art comes from the heart, from a place of passion and love."

Suraj couldn't hold back his tears. Chandini had been his mentor, his friend, and his biggest supporter. She had believed in him when no one else did.

Chandini continued, "Promise me, dear Suraj, that you will never stop creating. Your art has the power to inspire and bring joy to people's lives. Keep sharing your gift with the world, and you'll touch countless souls."

Suraj nodded with a heavy heart because he knew he would soon be losing a mentor and a wonderful friend. "I promise, Chandini. Your legacy will live on through my art."

With those words, Chandini closed her eyes, a peaceful smile on her face. She had passed on her wisdom and her belief in Suraj, leaving him with a sense of purpose and determination that burned brighter than ever.

In the days that followed, Chandini's condition worsened, and on a quiet morning, she took her last breath. The village was saddened by the loss of a beloved friend, a kind-hearted person, and a great mentor, but they also honoured her life and the profound impact she had on Suraj and the entire community.

# CHAPTER 6: THE ART OF INSPIRATION

Suraj had an overwhelming feeling of loss in the days that followed Chandini's loss of life. Her wisdom and guidance had been a constant presence in his life, and he missed her more than words could explain.

But he also knew that Chandini's belief in him had lit a fire within his heart. He couldn't let her memory fade away. Instead, he channelled his grief into his art, creating pieces that celebrated her spirit and the lessons she had taught him.

Word of Chandini's passing, and Suraj's heartfelt art reached everywhere. People travelled long distances to see Suraj's talent and to hear the story of an incredible mentoring between a young boy and a wise woman.

Suraj's art became a source of inspiration for others. It showed them that true art came from the heart, and that passion and dedication could overcome any challenge. Chandini's legacy lived on through Suraj's creations, touching the souls of those who viewed his work.

As the years went by, Suraj's art continued to evolve. He painted the beauty of the world around him, capturing the changing seasons, the vibrant colours of nature, and the emotions of the human spirit.

His painting mirrored the teachings he had learned from Chandini, such as the value of following one's dreams and the power of believing in oneself.

Suraj's dream of becoming a successful artist had become a reality, and he knew that Chandini's belief in him had played a significant role in his journey. Her memory lived on not only in his heart but in the hearts of all those who had been touched by his artwork.

And so, the story of Suraj's courageous journey, from a young boy with a dream to a successful artist, became a timeless tale that inspired generations. It taught them that with passion, determination, and the support of those who believed in you, even the loftiest dreams could be achieved.

As you embark on your own journey, remember Suraj's story. Let it remind you that within the simplest of materials and the deepest of dreams, lies the power to transform your life and inspire others. The courageous journey begins with a single step, taken with a heart full of hope.

# CHAPTER 7: THE ARTISTIC LEGACY

Years passed, and Suraj's reputation as a talented artist continued to grow. He held exhibitions in cities everywhere, showcasing his breathtaking paintings inspired by the beauty of nature and the lessons he had learned from Chandini.

People from all walks of life admired his creations, and his art had a way of touching their emotions. But amidst the success, Suraj remained humble, never forgetting the simple forest where he had first discovered his passion for art, nor the wise woman who had believed in him when no one else did.

## *AUTHOR'S NOTE:*

*SURAJ'S STORY TEACHES US NOT TO FORGET THE PEOPLE WHO HAVE HELPED US IN OUR LIVES. IT'S IMPORTANT TO REMEMBER WHERE WE STARTED AND HOW WE BEGAN. SHOWING GRATITUDE TO THOSE WHO HAVE HELPED YOU IN LIFE CAN BRIGHTEN THE PLACE AROUND YOU.*

One sunny morning, as Suraj walked through the familiar woods that had been his artistic sanctuary, he came across a group of children from the village. They gathered around a wooden easel and tried to emulate his style by using twigs, leaves, and stones.

Suraj greeted them with a smile and said, "The art you're creating is amazing." Remember, it's not about the materials; it's about the love you put into it."

The children looked up with wide eyes, their faces filled with admiration. One of them asked, "Were you the one who used to make art like this in the forest?" Suraj chuckled warmly, "Yes, that was me a long time ago."

The children were fascinated, and Suraj spent the day teaching them some of the techniques he had learned from Chandini. He hoped that, like Chandini had done for him, he could inspire the next generation of artists.

As the sun began to set, the children returned to their home with their newfound knowledge and a spark of creativity in their eyes. Suraj watched them go, feeling a deep sense of fulfilment. He knew that he was carrying on Chandini's legacy by nurturing the artistic dreams of others.

# CHAPTER 8: AN UNEXPECTED JOURNEY

One evening, Suraj received an unexpected letter while he was putting the finishing touches on a new painting. It was an invitation to an international art competition in a far-off city. In addition, the competition gave him the chance to show off his work on a worldwide scale.

Suraj was filled with excitement and anxiety. He had never been far from the village, and it was hard for him to imagine competing against artists from all over the world. But he also remembered Chandini's words, that life is full of tests and faith.

Suraj's heart was filled with determination, and he decided to accept the invitation. He was aware that the journey would be difficult, but he couldn't refuse the chance to share his art with a wider audience.

The villagers offered him their support and encouragement from behind. They had faith in Suraj, just as Chandini had in him. They believed in Suraj, just as Chandini had believed in him. With their blessings and Chandini's guidance, he set off on his journey to a city that was far away.

# CHAPTER 9: THE JOURNEY CONTINUES

Suraj's journey to the international art/painting competition included both new events and challenges. He took a train to explore lively cities and meet exceptional individuals and their traditions from different cultures and origins.

He was inspired by his surroundings every step of the way, sketching scenes in his notebook, and securing ideas for future paintings.

Upon arrival at the competition location, he was greeted by a magnificent display of art from all corners of the world.

The talent and creativity on display were awe-inspiring, and Suraj couldn't help but feel a sense of self-doubt. While creating his own artwork, he remembered Chandini's words and the support of his village community.

He was aware that his art was a reflection of his heart, and that was something that no one else could replicate.

The competition was rigorous, with judges inspecting every piece of work.
Suraj's paintings, which were a combination of nature's beauty and human emotions, touched many people.

They noticed that he had a unique perspective and a connection to the heart in his work.

Suraj was recognized as one of the winners. He was not only recognized, but also given the chance to display his work on a global scale.

The audience's applause and cheers showed the power of art to bridge cultures and touch souls.

# CHAPTER 10: A WORLD OF INSPIRATION

After the international art competition, Suraj's art gained global recognition. He travelled to different countries, displaying his work and meeting artists from diverse backgrounds.

He was inspired by the people he met and the places he visited, and his art continued to evolve, reflecting the richness of human experiences.

Suraj was surrounded by fame and success, but he never forgot his roots. He returned to his village as often as he could, telling stories about his successes and motivating the next generation of artists.

The children who had once watched him create art in the forest now looked up to him as a source of inspiration and hope.

Suraj's art had become a bridge that connected people from all walks of life. It reminded them of the beauty of the natural world, the importance of following their dreams, and the power of believing in oneself. And so, the story of Suraj's courageous journey continued, not only as a testament to the power of art but as a reminder that true success came from the heart, from a place of passion, determination, and the unwavering belief in one's dreams.

As you embark on your own journey, remember Suraj's story. Let it be a source of inspiration, reminding you that within the simplest of materials and the deepest of dreams, lies the power to transform your life and inspire others.

The courageous journey begins with a single step, taken with a heart full of hope.

# CHAPTER 11: THE ART OF GIVING BACK

As Suraj's art continued to flourish on the international stage, he never lost sight of the village that had nurtured his dreams.
With each exhibition and recognition, he received, he made it a point to give back to his community.

One summer, he organised an art camp for the village children. It was a week filled with creativity and imagination, where the children had the chance to explore their artistic talents just as Suraj had done in the forest years ago.

He taught them that art was not only about perfection but about expressing oneself from the heart.

The children embraced the opportunity with enthusiasm, and Suraj watched with pride as they created their own unique artworks. He saw Chandini's legacy living on through the young artists, just as it had through him.

Another winter, he used the proceeds from one of his exhibitions to show a scholarship fund for aspiring artists in the village.

The fund provided art supplies and educational opportunities to those who, like Suraj, had a burning passion for art but lacked the means to pursue it.

Through these acts of giving back, Suraj ensured that the village stayed a place where dreams could be nurtured, and artistic talents could flourish.

His success had become a source of inspiration not only for the children but for the entire community.

# CHAPTER 12: A RETURN TO ROOTS

Despite his global travels and recognition, Suraj always found solace in the forest where his artistic journey had begun. It was there, amidst the rustling leaves and chirping birds, that he felt most connected to his art and to Chandini's memory.

One autumn day, as the leaves painted the forest floor in shades of gold and red, Suraj returned to the very spot where he had met Chandini. He set up his easel, just as he had done as a young boy, and began to paint.

His brush moved with a sense of purpose, capturing the beauty of the changing season.

The trees appeared to come to life on his painting, and he sensed Chandini's presence alongside him, guiding his hand with each stroke.

As he painted, a group of villagers who had followed him into the forest watched in amazement.

They saw not only the beauty of his art but the deep connection he had to the place that had shaped his artistic soul.

One of the villagers approached Suraj and said, "Your art has touched our lives in ways we could never have imagined. You've shown us that dreams can come true, even for those from a small village."

Suraj smiled, his heart overflowing. "It's not just my art; it's the community's support and belief that has made it all possible.

"Without each and every one of you, I would not be where I am today."

Suraj had finished his painting, a masterpiece that captured the essence of the forest as well as the spirit of the village. It was a tribute to the place that had inspired him and the people who had believed in him.

# CHAPTER 13: A TIMELESS INSPIRATION

As the years passed, Suraj's painting has continued to inspire people all over the world. He gathered people from all walks of life, and his work found a permanent place in museums and galleries.

But Suraj's greatest satisfaction came from the knowledge that his art had touched the lives of countless individuals, in the same way that Chandini's belief had touched.

He received letters and messages from people who had found hope, inspiration, and a renewed passion for life through his paintings.

One day, a letter arrived at his doorstep. A young artist from a distant country wrote to him, saying,

"Your story and your art have shown me that dreams are worth pursuing, no matter where you come from. You've given me the courage to follow my own artistic path."

Suraj, touched by the message. In response he wrote a letter saying, "Believe in your dreams and create from your heart. Your art has the power to inspire and change lives. Remember, it's not about where you start; it's about where you're headed." He sent her a painting, a gift to fuel her artistic journey.

With those words, he continued to mentor and support artists from around the world, just as Chandini had mentored him. He knew that art had the ability to transcend boundaries and connect people on a deeper level.

Through his mentorship and outreach, Suraj saw the growth of a global community of artists inspired by his story and fuelled by the belief that his creativity could make a difference.

He came to the realisation that art was a universal language that could make a difference with one painting or story at a time. Suraj realised that his journey had become something much more significant than he had ever imagined. He had gone beyond the walls and become a bridge between hearts and nations through his painting, a tribute to the ever-lasting power of passion, determination, and self-belief.

Suraj continued to create, inspire, and convey the eternal message that lies inside the simplest of materials and the deepest of dreams, the ability to transform lives and touch hearts.

He understood that the courageous journey was a journey of giving, spreading hope, and connecting with kindred spirits around the world.

And as long as there were dreamers willing to pick up a brush and paint their stories, the inspiration born from his own courageous journey would live on, an eternal flame in the world of art.

# CHAPTER 14: THE LEGACY ENDURES

Suraj's art institution flourished into a vibrant centre of creativity, attracting young artists from everywhere, and the village continued to develop.

Dreams were encouraged, ideas were freely exchanged, and the spirit of Chandini and Suraj's journey lived on throughout the village.

The institute had grown into a haven for those eager to express themselves through art. Under Suraj's directive, students discovered the power of their own voices and the endless possibilities of their chosen medium.

They painted, sculpted, and produced with boundless excitement, knowing that their work carried the village's legacy as well as Chandini and Suraj's knowledge.

But it wasn't just the desired artists who felt the impact of the institute. The entire village had been transformed into a thriving group of art fans and supporters.

The streets were decorated with sculptures, murals, and colourful banners.

Once a basic structure, it is now lifting the pride of a great art that has surfaced on the wall, telling the story of Suraj's courageous journey and the village's never-ending spirit. Every year, villagers hosted an art exhibition that brought spectators from all over the world. It was a celebration of creation, a monument to the enduring power of dreams, and a reminder that greatness can be found in the humblest of places.

All the artwork which was displayed in the exhibition was not only made by the institute's students, but also the artists from all over the world who were inspired by Suraj's story.

It was an exhibition of various expertise and an acknowledgment to the world's interconnectedness through art.

As he walked through the vibrant exhibition of art, Suraj couldn't help but feel a strong feeling of fulfilment. Sometimes, he himself couldn't believe it as he came a long way from being that young boy in the forest. He also knew that his journey wasn't over.

He continued to tell his story to all the people who have inspired him and inspire people he met to be innovative.

Suraj's work and the village's heritage have become intertwined into the fabric of the village and the lives of its people.

Chandini's wisdom had left a permanent mark on their hearts, and Suraj's paintings served as a reminder that dreams might be realised through passion and determination.

Villages' legacy was continued through each stroke of a brush and every sculpture shaped by skilled hands.

An eternal expression of gratitude for the belief in the power of art, community, and the courageous journey of the human spirit.

The artworks and faces of those who gathered to celebrate were lit up by a warm, golden glow as the sun set over the village. Suraj was aware that his story had become a timeless tale of inspiration and hope.

It was a story that went beyond generations, a story that whispered to the hearts of dreamers.

A story that will endure as long as there are individuals willing to take the first courageous step towards their own dreams.

And so, as the stars appeared one by one in the night sky, Suraj continued to paint, to inspire, and to carry the torch of creativity that had ignited his journey so many years ago.

In the village, there was a legacy that remained, and the canvas of dreams was always open to those who dared to dream and create.

# CHAPTER 15: THE ARTISTIC CIRCLE

As Suraj's fame as an artist grew, he began to see a beautiful cycle forming. He now had the opportunity to inspire and guide young artists, just as Chandini had believed in him and inspired his artistic spark.

As the years went by, more and more young people came to learn the magic of art. Suraj had become a mentor! He continued to guide the students with kindness and patience that Chandini had shown him.

In the big studio of the institute, you could see students hunched over easels, their brushes dancing on canvases. Some were creating beautiful landscape paintings, while others were creating detailed sculptures.

As mentioned earlier, it was a place where ideas were freely shared, and everyone supported one another.

On a bright afternoon, Suraj sat with his students and was impressed by their work. They came from different backgrounds, each with a unique story to tell through their art. There was Lily, a young girl who was fascinated by colours, and Tim, a quiet boy who expressed his thoughts through sculpture. Suraj knew that art had a unique power. It could let people convey their feelings and communicate their stories without the use of words.

And he encouraged his students to do the same: to paint their dreams, sculpt their goals, and let their imaginations soar.

But it wasn't just the art that was important. It was all about the friendships that bloomed within those studio walls. Students became like a family, cheering on each other's triumphs and supporting one other's dreams. Their shared experiences included laughter, challenges, and, most significantly, a deep love for art.

One day, Suraj decided to organise an exhibition that displayed the work of his students. This was an opportunity for them to display their talents to the people in the village and the world.

The students' excitement in the air was palpable as they carefully selected their best pieces to display.

The exhibition was a tremendous success. The artwork was admired by people from the village and neighbouring towns. The room was filled with admiration from visitors as the walls were decorated with colourful paintings.

The students felt proud and realised that their dreams were coming true.

Suraj approached the students and expressed his state of happiness. The students began thanking Suraj for his mentorship role as they were given the chance to grow and shine. He knew Chandini would be pleased with what they had accomplished. The village's artistic culture rose to prominence, with each generation passing along their love of art and belief in dreams.

The place was where artists of all ages gathered to create, inspire, and celebrate the beauty of the human imagination.

So, Suraj's journey's legacy lived on in the warm embrace of the art institute, surrounded by the vibrant colours of creativity.

Not only in his own art, but also in the hearts and canvases of exceptional young artists who have proven themselves in the world of art.

# CHAPTER 16: A TIME OF REFLECTION

As the years flowed like a gentle river, Suraj found himself spending more time in quiet reflection.

He knew that he had achieved more than he could have ever imagined when he was that young boy in the village. Mentoring emerging talent and instilling a love for art in the hearts of young artists.

It was a source of pride and satisfaction for Suraj, knowing that he had played a vital role in shaping the dreams of so many.

He headed to the forest on a regular basis, not just to paint but also to sit under the familiar trees and listen to the wind's whispers.

The place was peaceful, and the gentle hum of nature's symphony surrounded him. Here, he could reflect on the path he had travelled and the impact he had made.

Chandini, the wise woman who had been his guiding light, was in his thoughts. Her teachings and belief in him led him to this remarkable journey.

He knew that she was with him in spirit, just as the forest was always with him in his art.

He also thought about the students he had mentored over the years. They had become like family to him, and their growth as artists had brought him great satisfaction.

Suraj's heart was filled with gratitude. He had a sense that his journey was not finished, that there were still stories to tell and dreams to inspire.

So, with a smile on his face, he gone ahead to paint the canvas of life, one stroke at a time, knowing that the village's legacy would live on through the dreams of those he had touched.

# CHAPTER 17: THE FINAL MASTERPIECE

As the years passed, Suraj's art became a source of inspiration for people all over the world. His paintings were displayed in prestigious museums, and his name was well-known to art lovers all over the world.

Suraj on the other hand, understood that his most important work was still ahead of him, discretely waiting in the depths of his imagination.

One bright morning, while sipping tea in his cozy studio, an idea began to form in Suraj's mind. His idea was to create a painting that would capture the essence of his life's journey, a painting that would be his final masterpiece. With a newfound enthusiasm, he gathered his brushes, paints, and a fresh canvas. People in the village have always been his inspiration, and he wanted to capture its spirit like never before this time.

The painting would be a rousing celebration of life, a mosaic of colours and emotions that had shaped his courageous journey.

It would tell the story of a young boy who discovered his passion in the forest and emerged into a well-known artist while still being obedient to his roots.

Suraj began with a backdrop of a lush forest with tall trees reaching for the sky. The leaves were a vibrant mix of greens, each shade chosen carefully to convey the changing seasons.

It was a reference to the place where everything started, where Chandini's wisdom had ignited his artistic passion.

In the foreground, he painted a path that was winding, a symbol of the journey he had taken. Through the fields of wildflowers, it passed through moments of growth, learning, and discovery.

While painting, he couldn't help but smile, reminiscing about the people and experiences that had shaped him.

He showed young artists working among the flowers, their faces filled with enthusiasm and commitment. The students he had mentored were the next generation of dreamers who would continue the village's tradition.

Their work brought vibrancy and depth to the canvas, just as they brought depth to his life.

But the centrepiece of the painting was a figure seated in the forest, an elderly Suraj. He painted himself as a man who was both wise and content, surrounded by the beauty he had cherished all his life.

In his hand, he held a paintbrush, forever connected to the art that had defined him.

The forest reflected the sky's colours, resulting in a mesmerising blend of blues and purples. The symbol of reflection was the quiet moments he had spent contemplating the meaning of his journey.

The towering trees surrounded the forest, their branches creating a protective canopy, just as Chandini had been his protector and guide. As Suraj added the final strokes to the canvas, a sense of completion washed over him.

This painting was not just a reflection of his life; it was a tribute to the village that had nurtured him, the mentor who had inspired him, and the students who had become his family.

The final masterpiece proved how art can transcend time and bring people together. It was a reminder that every brush stroke, every sculpture, and every creative endeavour had the power to create a lasting impression, touch hearts, and inspire future generations.

Suraj knew that his courageous journey had reached its ultimate expression when the painting was finished. It was a journey of following dreams, believing in oneself, and the profound connection between art and the human spirit.

He felt a tremendous feeling of tranquillity as he gazed at the canvas. His legacy extended beyond his art to the people he touched and the inspiration he sparked.

The masterpiece that had been created was a gift to the world, a sign of hope, and a reminder that the canvas of life was limitless, waiting for each person to paint their own courageous journey.

# CHAPTER 18: THE LEGACY LIVES ON

Time had a way of moving forward, Suraj saw the village's evolution and growth. It is the spirit of creativity and belief in the power of dreams that remains unchanged.

On the other hand, Suraj's legacy remained vibrant throughout the village. The final masterpiece he created is still on the walls of the community centre, a tribute of his perseverance and the spirit of the village.

He was well aware that his career as an artist was coming to an end, but he also knew the legacy he had established. His legacy of enthusiasm, determination, and self-belief will continue in the many lives he has touched.

A few days later, a group of youngsters gathered at the community centre, and Suraj's story was a visual treat for them.

"Give us some insights, Grandpa," one of the children pleaded, tugging at an elderly man's sleeve.

The elderly man was none other than Suraj himself, his white hair and kind smile reflecting the way of life. When Suraj began to speak, the children visualised themselves in the forest, discovering their own passions. Suraj saw it as a moment of passing the torch, of ensuring that the village's legacy lived on in the hearts of the next generation.

On a particular day, a group of artists from another country came to the village. They heard about Suraj's story and wanted to honour the artist who had touched many lives. Suraj greeted them warmly and took them on a tour of his studio.

One of the visiting artists, a young woman named Radha, approached Suraj with tears in her eyes. Although she spoke in a language that was foreign to him, her emotions overwhelmed her words.

Suraj's journey had a major impact on Radha's art, and she wanted to express her gratitude.

With a smile, Suraj took Radha's hand and led her to a blank canvas. He gave her a brush, and they started painting together. It was a silent conversation, a meeting of souls through art.

Suraj's strokes intermingled perfectly with Radha's, resulting in an excellent piece of art that expressed a story of connection, shared dreams, and the universal language of creativity.

Radha's tears turned into smiles and the villagers were shocked. They realised that Suraj's legacy had transcended borders and languages, and his art had the power to bring people from all over the world.

One peaceful evening, Suraj closed his eyes with a feeling of contentment, surrounded by the beauty he had enjoyed his entire life. He felt a great connection to the world, to the people he had inspired, and to the dreams that continued to flourish in people's hearts.

As you embark on your own journey, remember Suraj's story. Take it as a source of inspiration, reminding you that no dream is too big or any obstacle too daunting when you are fuelled by passion, determination, and unwavering belief in yourself.

# CONCLUSION

"The Courageous Journey" encourages everyone who reads it to follow their own path, find support from others, be brave in pursuing aspirations, and recognize that art is a language that everyone can understand. It's a story about community, wisdom, and how creativity can transform the world.

www.ingramcontent.com/pod-product-compliance
Lightning Source LLC
Chambersburg PA
CBHW040103150726
48005CB00013B/1560